A HUGE HOLLYWOOD MYSTERY IN A QUIET ENGLISH VILLAGE

LILY MCGEE COZY MYSTERIES
BOOK ONE

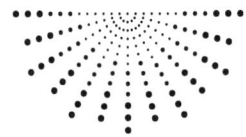

DONNA DOYLE

PUREREAD.COM

CONTENTS

Prologue	1
Chapter 1	7
Chapter 2	19
Chapter 3	27
Chapter 4	43
Chapter 5	56
Epilogue	61
What's next for Lily?	67
Other Books In This Series	83
Our Gift To You	85

PROLOGUE

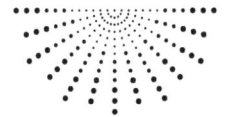

Lily McGee rushed through the movie studio, dodging errant props and other people along the way. Her honey brown hair was pulled back in a tight ponytail, but strands had come loose and were falling around her heart-shaped face. Her cheeks were rosy, her eyes sharp, and her heart was pounding as she felt the pressure of time crushing her. Panting for breath, she reached the shadowed set and ran toward the director, Howard Boxall. Huge cameras stood behind the director, watching the set from different angles, while others on the crew looked on. Howard was standing there with his star, Rick Chambers. The two men were complete opposites of each other. Rick was the handsome, classic Hollywood archetype of a leading man while Howard was a squinting, wispy haired, narrow faced auteur who had made a career of being difficult, and brilliant. Currently, Rick had the script in his hand and was glaring at Howard, looming over him like death itself, not that Howard was intimidated. The director had his neck arched back and hands on his hips, fury pouring out of his eyes.

"You can write this stuff Howard, but you sure as shooting can't say it!" Rick fumed.

"You'll say whatever I want you to say. What, do you think because you're on the cover of magazines, the world's prettiest man, that you know better than me?"

"I know what the people want Howard. That's why my box office takings are gold and yours are... well... let's just say there's a reason why the studio wanted me on this picture. Your best days are behind you."

Howard narrowed his eyes. "I've had more good days than you've had witless teenagers fawning over you, and let's not forget that genius lasts forever while looks fade. You should be lucky you can make money while you can."

Rick threw his head back and laughed, shaking his head. Lily watched on meekly. Confrontations like these had been a regular occurrence on the film set and certainly wasn't anything like what she expected when she had taken the job as Howard's personal assistant. She assumed it would afford her the opportunity to work closely with a visionary director and benefit from his creative wisdom, instead she had been faced with a petty man whose cruelty surpassed anything else. Even the set had not been as exciting as she had hoped. It was mostly filled with surly faces. The glitz and glamor of Hollywood was as much of an illusion as anything else on the screen.

"What do you want?" Howard asked sharply, his gaze sweeping away from Rick.

"I just came with your coffee," Lily replied gently. She was almost thirty, yet when Howard spoke to her she felt like a misbehaving child.

"Finally," the director barked as he snatched the coffee from her. "I don't know why it took you so long to get back to me. He took a hearty gulp and then grimaced. "What the heck is this? I didn't ask for it cold," he spat in disgust. "I've had it with this place. What happened to the good old days?" he growled as he threw the coffee away. Lily assumed that he meant to throw it on the floor, but if that was the case then his aim was amiss because it hit Lily, right in the chest. The cold coffee (which wasn't as cold as Howard claimed it to be and left an uncomfortable warmth seeping over her chest) burst over her, leaving her shocked. Howard and Rick stormed away in different directions, leaving Lily to stare into the blank cameras that saw everything, sopping wet and forlorn.

Joanie rushed up to her, blonde tresses bouncing with every step, pink lipstick glowing like a neon sign.

"Oh my gosh Lily, are you okay?"

Lily's lips were a thin line and her tone was flat. "I've had it Joanie. I'm out of here. Lily McGee's love affair with Hollywood is over."

Lily had no idea where she was going or what she was going to do next. All she knew was that she needed a new start.

CHAPTER ONE

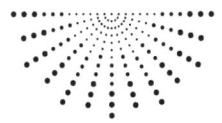

Lily McGee threw open the wide windows of her cottage and breathed in the sweet air of the English countryside. A small rock wall separated the grounds of her cottage from the winding lane that led to the heart of Didlington St. Wilfrid. Rolling fields rose toward the horizon, framed by trimmed hedges and populated by fluffy sheep. There was not a hint of smog in the sky. When she closed her eyes she was immersed in silence. Exhaling softly, she sighed with relief. The busy, bustling world of Hollywood was far away, and with it so too were all of her stress levels. She brought a slice of toast that was coated with jelly, although she told herself that she was going to have to get used to calling it jam, to her lips. The taste was rich and luxurious. The sky was pale blue, the scenery idyllic. She felt blessed for being able to be in a cottage like this. The rent was similar to what she had paid for a squat, blocky apartment in Los Angeles. Here she had the freedom of space, the luxury of solitude, and she didn't have to put up with the bumps and thumps of her neighbors. Nor was she plagued with the sound of police sirens. This village was quaint, quiet, and exactly what Lily needed to recharge her batteries after being drained by the rigors of Hollywood.

After finishing her breakfast she went to the small study where she opened her laptop and settled down for a day of writing. As blessed as she felt to live here, her savings would only last for so long, so she needed to find a way to earn money. She turned to doing something she had always wanted to do; write cozy mysteries. This village seemed like the perfect place to get a lot of writing done since it was quiet and free of distractions, but as she settled into her seat and stared at the blank document in front of her she realized that she needed something else; she needed inspiration.

Lily rested her fingers against the keys, tapping out a rhythm in the hope it would conjure an idea from the depths of her mind. She looked all around the room, as though the magic idea was lurking in a corner somewhere like a spider, and then she gazed out of the window. Clouds idly drifted by and they seemed to take form before her eyes, but only in the shapes of animals. She leaned back and pinched the bridge of her nose, trying to figure out where to start and where to end, and what to put in between. The more she stared at the document the more foreboding it seemed, as though it was a white abyss that threatened to swallow her. She muttered under her breath and rubbed her eyes.

"At this rate it'll only take me about, oh, fifty years to write one novel."

She tapped her fingers against the table and then shook her head. Whatever she needed wasn't going to happen in this one room. Rising, she ran a hand through her hair and made her way out of the cottage. Closing the door behind her, she looked at the etching of a bird on a plaque and the words 'Starling Cottage'. There were a number of cottages dotted around the village, all owned by Lord Huntingdon, who was renting them out. He must have had an interest in birds as they were all named after different types.

A winding path led to a small road that was framed with colorful flowers. The scent in the air was sweet and she strolled along, hoping that she would catch sight of something that would inspire her. The creative process had always been something that intrigued her. It was like alchemy in a way, creating something from nothing, and she had hoped that by working in Hollywood she would glean some sense to help her own process. Unfortunately all the people she had known were difficult and saw her as a nuisance more than anything else. There wasn't much she missed about the life, apart from Joanie. Friends had been few and far between, and for all her faults Joanie had been there when it mattered.

After she had been walking for a little while, the aroma of freshly baked bread drifted toward her and pulled her toward the bakery, which was owned by a woman called Marjorie Porter. She was a plump woman with a ruddy face, a cheery disposition, and a bob of curly hair. The picture of her husband, the dearly departed Henry, hung on the wall. This bakery had been a frequent stop of Lily's since she had moved in, although she had to control herself because she knew that she would balloon up if she didn't. It was easy to stay slender in Hollywood, what with the long and draining working hours, squirreling away something to eat only when chance allowed. The hours were long here, and there were plenty of opportunities to indulge her appetites.

"What can I get for you today Lily?" Marjorie asked. Lily was still getting used to the personal touch. People around here had gotten used to her quickly because she was new, and because she was from far away.

"I'm not sure. I just came in here to look really," Lily said, and her mouth began to salivate when she saw the currant buns, the éclairs, and the iced cakes that Marjorie had baked. "Actually I told myself that I need to be more disciplined around you. I'm already beginning to get a little too comfortable," she patted her belly and laughed. Marjorie chuckled as well.

"I don't agree with that. I think you need a little meat on your bones if you're going to attract a husband."

Lily offered a wan smile. "That's not really at the top of my list of priorities."

"You say that now, but you never know when you're going to meet the right person. I'm surprised you never settled down with one of those famous actors since you lived in Hollywood."

"Believe me, they might be handsome, but they're rarely charming," Lily said. The truth was that she hadn't exactly mixed with the higher echelons of Hollywood, but the people of this village believed otherwise.

"Well you just keep your eyes peeled because you never know when you're going to meet someone. And don't be afraid to enjoy life. The worst thing you can do is miss out on all the small pleasures." She said this as she reached in and brought out an iced bun with some tongs, placing it in a paper bag. Lily hadn't remembered ordering it, but she found that it was exactly what she was in the mood for.

When she left the bakery she pondered Marjorie's words. She certainly hadn't given much thought to romance as the possibilities out here were few and far between. After some car crashes of romance back in Hollywood it was refreshing to not have the pressure of it all on her mind. For the time being she wanted to focus on herself and her books. If she was going to meet someone then it would happen in its good time. For now she was just going to enjoy a bun.

While she was walking she continued to admire the scenery, which was so vivid and colorful it seemed unreal. She was used to the grey, drab color of city blocks and fences. This place only had the lightest human touch, and it was all the better for it. Lily was interrupted from her reverie by a fluffy black dog that bounded up to her. His pink tongue lolled out and his eyes were as brown as the trunk of an old tree.

"Hello boy," she laughed as the dog lifted itself on its hind legs and placed its paws on her waist. He was a medium sized dog, but in just the few moments she had interacted with him, Lily could tell that he had a lot of personality.

He was sniffing toward her fingers, which were still dusted with sugary icing from the bun she'd eaten. She pulled her hand away and laughed as the dog stretched itself to its maximum length in an effort to reach her fingers, as though the sweet taste was the only thing that mattered in his life. Most of his fur was black, but there was a white patch running from his right eye down his neck, leaving a tinge of white on his long, floppy ear.

"Zeus, get back here," a stern voice barked through the air, and was followed by a whistle. Lily looked up and saw a stocky man walking toward her. He had a salt and pepper beard, he wore a tweed jacket, and a flat cap.

"What a lovely dog," Lily said as the man drew closer.

"What would you know about it?" the man snapped. Lily was taken aback by the disgruntled manner of the man. Most people had been pleasant when she encountered them and it had been a nice change from the city, but it seemed as though ill manners had found their way into this idyllic place as well.

"Excuse me?" Lily asked.

The man stopped in his tracks and clicked his hands, commanding Zeus to stay by his side. The dog sat there happily.

"I don't know what you want here, but you're not welcome."

"What I want? I'm sorry… but have you gotten me confused with someone else?"

"No, I haven't, not as long as you're that American writer who is coming along to make fools of us all?"

"I'm a writer yes, but I don't know where you've heard this. I don't want to make a fool out of anyone."

"That's what they all say," he grunted, shaking his head. "I know your type. You come here thinking that we're simple folk, and you want the whole world to laugh at us. Others might look at you and treat you like you're some kind of visiting royalty, but we're just a tourist attraction to you. We're real people, with real lives, and I'm not going to have you make us look like idiots."

Lily was left aghast. Before she could apologize and reason with the man to try and understand what had provoked this intense outburst, he was already marching away with his dog in tow. She wasn't sure she had ever seen more of a difference between an owner and their pet before, and she was left wondering what had caused the chip to appear on his shoulder.

The interaction brought back memories of her encounter with Howard and how he had berated her. It made her wonder what would happen if Howard had come to a place like this rather than her. Surely the irascible man would have clashed with the local population. A smile twitched on her face and suddenly she forgot all about the unpleasant meeting with the stranger. Inspiration had struck! She finally had her idea, and she raced back to

Starling Cottage, flinging herself into her chair where her fingers typed so fast they became a blur.

An arrogant Hollywood director would come to a quiet English village to shoot a movie and end up infuriating one of the locals. It drew on her own experiences, and was something that she could sink her teeth into. After all, she figured that she might as well get *something* out of her Hollywood career.

CHAPTER TWO

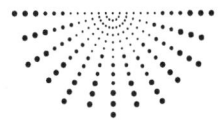

Lily had been writing consistently for about two weeks. The words flowed from her mind and she was proud of herself for writing so much. She took a little too much joy in writing the murder scene as she worked through some lingering frustration with Howard. She didn't *mean* it to resemble him as much as it did, but it just happened that he fit the character she wanted to write about. She grinned as she turned over different plots in her mind and developed the suspects. It seemed so fitting, and she liked that the story had some meat to it. In her mind it wasn't simply a mystery, rather it was a way to tell the story of the modern age, of huge cities clashing with a simpler way of life. In truth it was something that she was caught between as well. She had spent all her life in the city, and while moving to Didlington St. Wilfrid was a nice change of pace she wasn't sure if she would want to spend her entire life here. Still, there was time for all that when and if she got her book published. For now she needed to focus on the writing of it.

To reward herself for such good work she found herself popping into Marjorie's bakery again, and was greeted with a smile. After selecting a few sweet treats to take home with her, Lily decided to ask Marjorie about the ill-tempered man she had encountered two weeks earlier.

Marjorie arched her eyebrows and sighed. "Ah yes, that sounds like Pat."

"Well what's his problem?" Lily asked.

"Who knows with Pat? He's not exactly the type to talk about his feelings, although if you ask me not many men learn that skill. He lives up on the old farm and keeps to himself. It's just him and Zeus you know, for as long as I can remember. I think he just doesn't like outsiders. I wouldn't worry about him though. Most people here like a bit of excitement and you've certainly provided that!"

"I have?" Lily asked quizzically, surprised that she had had such an impact on the small village.

"Oh yes," Marjorie drew in a gasp. "Everyone is talking about you. We rarely get anything exciting happening around here. I think you should give a talk at the community hall. I'm sure you must have so many amazing stories to tell. It's not as though people here get to travel that much. Some of us dream of leaving but, well…" she sighed and trailed off. Lily wondered where Marjorie's dreams would have taken her, and if it was her love that had rooted her to this place. Lily's eyes drifted to the picture of Marjorie's husband and wondered what it would be like to love someone so much you were willing to stay in one place.

"I'm sure I'm not all that exciting," Lily said dryly. In Hollywood nobody had ever paid any attention to her, and she had never been anything special. It was strange to think that people were talking about her behind her back and creating stories about her. "But I don't have anything to worry about from Pat or anyone else, do I?"

"Of course not," Marjorie chuckled. "Pat is Pat. He'd get angry at a passing cloud if it suited him, but he doesn't mean any harm. As for anyone else, well, they're just curious, that's all. It's not often that something unusual happens in our little corner of the world."

Lily wasn't too sure that Pat's anger should be taken for granted. It can't have done his disposition any good, but she hadn't arrived here to become a therapist so she thanked Marjorie for the kind words and departed from the bakery, carrying the sweet treats with her. She had been around many celebrities during her time in Hollywood, and it had never occurred to her that she would end up becoming one, but she supposed to these people she was a symbol of a life that they could only dream of. Little did they know that the dream was really a nightmare, and they were much better off here.

When Lily returned to the cottage she settled at her desk again and began to think of ideas for various other characters while eating the things she had picked up from the bakery. Marjorie really was a magician, and she wondered what other secrets were hiding in Didlington St. Wilfrid.

A while later, Lily was interrupted from her thoughts by a knock at the door. It took her a few moments to respond because she wasn't expecting anyone at all. She furrowed her brow, wondering if some interested villager had worked up the courage to visit her and possibly learn something about Hollywood.

But when she opened the door she saw someone she hadn't been expecting at all.

"Lily! It's been so long. Oh I've missed you so much!" Joanie exclaimed. She walked in, the air sweeping around her. Her smile was wide, her statuesque beauty somehow not quite fitting the quaint humility of the cottage. Her platinum blonde hair glowed, her lipstick shone, and she looked as though she belonged in another world. Joanie flung her arms around Lily's neck and squeezed her tightly, all while Lily was nonplussed.

"Look at this place, it's so cute! Oh my gosh it's like something out of a movie," Joanie moved away from Lily, leaving a suitcase standing in the doorway. She tilted her head back and gazed around in awe at Starling Cottage. Lily had to pinch herself to make sure that she hadn't fallen asleep.

"Joanie what are you doing here?" she asked in disbelief.

Joanie turned and flashed a wide, dazzling smile.

"I came here because I missed you of course! Life isn't the same without you Lily and I wanted to pay you a visit, make sure you're not getting yourself in any trouble. Of course, to do that I had to bring work with me."

Lily arched an eyebrow and her chest tightened with anxiety. "What do you mean you brought work with you?"

Joanie sidled toward Lily, draping an arm around her shoulder. "Well you know I couldn't really afford to take a vacation. Howard needed another location for the movie and I thought why not shoot it in a small English village? We're here to scout. There are only a few of us you know, but I thought it would be the perfect opportunity to see you again!"

"Howard is here?" Lily asked, her face turning ashen.

"Yes! Howard, Rick, Doug the camera guy, and a few other people. It's going to be like a big party!" I thought that I might stay with you to make things more fun. The others can all go somewhere else. It looks like you have the room," Joanie wandered through the cottage and made herself at home, murmuring appreciation for the place. Lily's throat was dry as she leaned against a wall and pressed her hand against her forehead. A band of tension suddenly knotted around the front of her face. She had come here to get away from Howard and Hollywood and everything that happened there. What had Joanie done?

Lily heard some commotion outside and walked down her garden path to see what was happening. There was a huge coach hissing as it tried to eke its way down a narrow lane, and Pat was there, shaking his fist at the vehicle. Lily rolled her eyes, knowing that this was only the beginning. Her peaceful idyll had just been disrupted and it was only going to get worse.

CHAPTER THREE

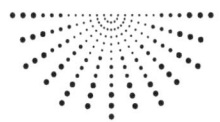

"Get away from here! What do you think you're doing bringing this monster down this lane, it's clearly not going to fit!" Pat yelled. His expression was twisted into a scowl and his cheeks were crimson. Zeus was circling him, swept up in the excitement. The windows of the coach were tinted and it looked a foreboding sight. The doors opened and Howard emerged. Lily groaned and started toward the two of them before war could break out, although she feared she was already too late.

"Get out of my way!" Howard yelled, storming toward Pat.

"What right do you have coming down here with this thing?"

"I have every right. I'm making a movie," Howard shot back, as though that explained everything. They were yelling at the top of their lungs and Lily grimaced as the peace was shattered. Zeus stood beside Pat, looking at the proceedings with intrigue. Howard was his usual brash self, caring only about himself and his movie.

"I'm sure that we can settle this matter without having to wake the entire village," Lily said upon reaching them. The two men looked at her with withering stares.

"You should keep out of it as well. You're as bad as them," Pat said.

"I have nothing to say to you," Howard added. "As far as I'm concerned you're dead to me. I only want loyal people around me, not people who are going to walk away at the first sign of stress."

His words cut Lily sharply. She gasped, for she hadn't left at the first sign of trouble at all, not that Howard would believe her.

Howard turned back to Pat. "Now get out of our way. We have every right to stay here. We've paid the fees to camp in the field. You should be fortunate that we picked this forgotten little place to make our movie. It's not as though this place has any significance otherwise," Howard spoke in a scathing tone, and then he turned to Lily. "It's no wonder why you wanted to retreat here. You get to hide away in this little corner of the world without having to do anything difficult. That's the problem with your generation. You don't know the meaning of hard work."

Before Lily could reply two figures had emerged from the coach. One was the star, Rick Chambers, while the other one was the camera man, Doug.

"Come on Howard, let's just get back on the coach," Rick said, turning to Pat. "I'm sorry sir, it's been a long flight and a long way to get here. We're all a little tired and stressed. This village is lovely and we're honored that you've allowed us into your home. We'll be gone before you know it, I promise, and then life can get back to normal."

His voice was as smooth as honey and Lily had to give him credit for being able to defuse the situation. He could be charming when he wanted to be, which she supposed was the gift of acting. After all, she had seen his temper flare at Howard as well. Just being around them for a few moments was enough to make a band of tension run around her forehead, and she was glad that she had made the decision to walk away.

"Come on Howard, let's go," Doug said, putting his arms around the director. Doug was a big, husky man, and like most people he towered over Howard.

"Get your hands off me," Howard said, shrugging away Doug's efforts to get him back on the coach. "The last thing I need is you treating me like some old fool. Just point the camera where I tell you. That's the only reason you're here," Howard snapped bitterly as he climbed the steps back into the coach. Doug rolled his eyes and Lily pitied him. Meanwhile, Rick was shaking Pat's hand and wore a warm smile on his face before he turned away. The moment he did, and the moment he was certain that Pat had been placated, that smile fell from his face and he scowled. Lily was convinced that there was going to be fireworks on that coach.

The coach hissed and trundled down the narrow road, moving slowly to avoid scraping the small stone walls that stood on either side of the path. Unfortunately there were a few plants and bushes that were squashed by the wide tires. Pat rolled his eyes and glared at Lily, but he didn't say anything else before moving on. She watched the coach as it drove toward a field, where it stopped and all the crew filtered out to begin building their camp that would be their home for the duration of the shoot.

She sighed as she returned to Starling cottage. Joanie was there waiting for her.

"Well, I'm glad you brought this storm with you," Lily said tersely.

Joanie wrung her hands. "I'm sorry, but I thought it would be a good way to get a free trip over here to see you! It's not like it's going to last forever either. You know what Howard is like, he likes to get his movies done quickly. I'm sure it's going to be over before you know it and then you can carry on with whatever you want to do here," she said.

Lily found it impossible to be angry with Joanie, but she hoped that Joanie spoke the truth. The last thing she needed was to have a film crew around the village interfering with the peace and quiet. She had come to Didlington St. Wilfried to escape Hollywood, not to bring it with her.

Still, interacting with Howard again gave her fuel for her story. The man inspired her in all the worst ways and the ideas began swimming in her mind. He managed to irritate almost everyone he met, and writing about his demise was strangely satisfying. She wrote long into the night, losing herself in her story until the hours were small.

Lily awoke to the sound of heavy knocking on her door. She groaned and rubbed her eyes, for sleep had been fleeting. Yawning, she walked to the door and wondered who could be calling for her at this time of the morning. She dreaded to think it might be Howard. Even though she had quit Hollywood he would probably demand that she continue working for him because that's the kind of man he was. However, she was surprised to see a police officer standing before her. He was a tall man with a ruddy complexion and a thick mustache sitting above his upper lip. His uniform was stretched tight around his rotund body, and his voice was deep and rasping.

"Are you Miss McGee?" he asked.

"I am," Lily replied, narrowing her eyes as she wondered what this was about.

"I'm Constable Dudley, Bob Dudley and I'd like to ask you a few questions if I may," he said.

"Of course. What is this about?"

Constable Dudley sucked in a breath and lowered his voice. "I'm afraid to tell you that there was a murder last night," he said.

"A murder?" Joanie replied, squealing loudly. Lily's eyes were wide with shock. Constable Dudley's eyes were wide as well, but not because of the murder, but because of Joanie's appearance. She was dressed in a robe which showed off her long, elegant legs and it must have been a sight that Constable Dudley had never seen before because he was quite distracted.

"What exactly happened? Who was murdered?" Lily asked, trying to get the Constable's attention back on the matter at hand.

"Ah, yes," Constable Dudley was flustered, but he managed to tear his gaze away from Joanie. "This is the reason why I'm here. The victim is Howard Boxall, the director of the film. I believe you knew him. I'm trying to ask anyone that knew him for any insight about the man. As you can imagine we don't get many murders around here, so I'm trying to get the case wrapped up quickly. Can you tell me about your relationship with him?"

"Howard was murdered? Lily, this sounds just like your story!" Joanie gasped.

Lily had been blinking slowly, trying to process the news that Howard had died. When Joanie said what she said, Lily glared at her.

"Excuse me? What story?" Constable Dudley asked.

"It's nothing really," Lily said, chuckling lightly because it was all a silly misunderstanding. "I left my career in Hollywood to come here and write murder mysteries. It's just a coincidence that I happened to base the first book on my own life."

"I see," the constable made a few notes in his little book. "And in this book it's the director of the film who died?"

"Yes," Lily admitted. "But it really is just a coincidence."

"And why did you choose the director? Did you have some kind of animosity toward him? Is that why you left Hollywood?"

Lily arched her eyebrows. Constable Dudley certainly didn't waste any time in getting to the heart of the matter. He reminded her of a battering ram, and was clearly eager to crash his way through to the truth.

"When you speak to more people I think you'll find that everyone had animosity with Howard. He was that type of person. He's a genius and his films have won many awards, but he's not a pleasant man to work with. He's very demanding and he has a volatile temper, but I promise you it wasn't I who killed him."

"I see," the constable said. He didn't sound convinced by her declaration of innocence, and she supposed it was the exact thing a guilty person would say. "The murder took place during the night. Could you tell me what you were doing?"

"I was writing until quite late, around midnight I think, and then I went to bed," Lily said.

"And can you corroborate this Miss…?" the Constable said, turning to Joanie.

"Joanie Dawson," Joanie strode across the room toward the door and took the Constable's hand, flashing him a warm smile.

His cheeks glowed an even brighter red and he muttered something unintelligible.

"Well Miss Dawson, were you in the house as well?"

"I was," she began, and then looked awkward, "but I'm afraid I was asleep so I didn't hear Lily come to bed. I take sleeping tablets you see because otherwise I simply can't get my mind to turn off and so I'm always out like a light. I'm sorry I can't be more help officer but I can assure you that Lily isn't the kind of person to do this. She's my best friend, but I'm sure you'll find out who the real murderer is. I just hope this isn't some kind of vendetta against people in the movie industry. What if we're targeted next," Joanie gasped.

"I'm sure you'll be safe. I'll get to the bottom of this soon enough," Constable Dudley puffed out his chest as he spoke.

"Where exactly did the murder take place?" Lily asked.

"In one of Lord Huntingdon's houses. I'm not sure what this director of yours was doing up there at that time of night, but I suppose he had his reasons."

"And how was he murdered?

"Well that's the strange thing," Constable Dudley scratched the back of his neck. "It seems as though history is repeating itself."

"What do you mean? I thought you said that there weren't any murders around here?" Lily asked, suddenly intrigued.

"I meant nowadays. But in the past there was a murder, a grisly one at that. It involved one of the Lord's ancestors. A terrible thing. One of the stable hands was in love with the Lord's daughter at the time, but she was promised to another. The betrothed husband was found dead in the same room as your director, also from a head wound, again, the same as your director."

"So you don't know exactly what killed him yet?" Lily asked.

"All I know is that it was something heavy. I still have a lot of questions I need to ask, and a lot of people I need to speak to. I appreciate all your help and, well, I'd advise you not to leave the village until the investigation is over." The constable spoke with a warning tone and Lily was able to infer that she was under suspicion, which was a frightening thought. She thanked him and the constable went about his business, while Lily closed the door and turned to face Joanie.

"I can't believe Howard is really dead," Joanie said with a look of shock upon her face. Now that Constable Dudley had left they were given the opportunity to properly process their grief, although Lily did have a few other things on her mind.

"I know. So many people have threatened to kill him over the years, but someone finally did it," Lily said.

"I'm sorry for being unable to lie to the cop for you. I thought it was better to be honest,"

Joanie offered a small smile, but Lily told her not to worry.

"I didn't do it so I'm not upset, although I don't like the fact that I'm under suspicion. If they can't find the actual murderer then I might be suspect number one. After all, it's not a leap of logic to suggest that I still hold enmity toward him, given I left Hollywood because of him. It would have been a shock to me to see him again, and we've already had another altercation. I think I'm going to have to try and find the real murderer before people start believing that I had anything to do with this." The more Lily thought about it the more afraid she was. In her heart she knew she was innocent, but that wouldn't matter to anyone else. She was writing a story where the director was dead and that meant all eyes were going to be on her, but if she didn't do it, then who did?

"Where are you going to start?" Joanie asked.

"I don't know, but the fact that this murder resembles a local legend makes me wonder if it was actually anyone on the film crew at all. After all, they all know how Howard is and if they haven't killed him yet why would they start now? I don't think we can discount the possibility that it's a local, and I think I know which one I want to talk to first."

CHAPTER FOUR

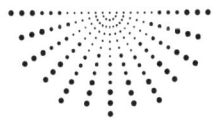

Lily was reeling from the news that Howard had died. Despite having a difficult relationship with him she never would have wished death upon him, especially not in such a grisly way. Still, she had to be pragmatic about the situation and acknowledge that Howard was the type of man who would create more enemies than friends, and not everyone was going to be willing to give him a pass for his genius. She had certainly not foreseen herself becoming involved in investigating an actual murder. Writing one was difficult enough, but she felt personally invested in this one because she knew the people involved, and now she was about to have a difficult conversation.

Lily made her way across a field toward an old farmhouse. A single wisp of smoke rose from a chimney. A pigsty was attached to the house, and elsewhere sheep roamed about the grass, grazing happily without a care in the world. The house was weathered and she imagined it must have been standing here for generations. She rapped her knuckles against the door and waited for it to open. Within moments Pat was there, with Zeus by his side as always. The contrast between the two greetings she got was huge. Zeus was happy to see her, nuzzling her hand and licking her fingers, while Pat stared at her with narrowed eyes.

"What do you want?" he asked gruffly.

"I just… I just wanted to speak to you about the murder that happened. Has Constable Dudley been to see you yet?"

"Of course he has, not that the fat headed fool has any idea what he's doing. He couldn't solve the crime if the murderer came right up to him with bloody hands and confessed. But what has it got to do with me?"

Lily flashed a smile, trying to put Pat at ease. She clasped her hands in front of her and spoke in her friendliest tone. "Well you may not know this but I'm actually writing a mystery story of my own and I suppose I'm trying to see how people have reacted to the news so that in my story I can make sure the reactions are genuine, and you being someone who recently had an altercation with Howard... well... I thought you might have some insight into the matter."

Pat barked a laugh. "You Hollywood types are all the same. Why say one word when a hundred will do? I know what this is about. You're getting bored and the moment something exciting happens you want to get involved. You think it's so simple don't you? The local man gets into an argument with an

American and then the American turns up dead. It makes sense, doesn't it? It's all neat and tidy and you wouldn't have to worry about anything else. Believe me, I have better things to do with my time than going around killing people I get into arguments with. All I want is to be left alone. I don't know who killed him and I don't particularly care. All I hope is that it means the lot of you will clear out and go back to wherever you came from. Now I'd appreciate it if you didn't come by here again. I don't particularly like opening my door and being accused of killing someone."

Before Lily could say anything else Pat had slammed the door in her face. She cringed at the way she had gone about things and certainly hadn't meant to accuse him outright, but she did wonder if his protestations were done to protect him. Pat didn't strike her as a daft man. He might well have seen an opportunity to kill a man and use the rest of the film crew as a shield. After all, there were many likelier killers who know Howard more intimately than Pat did. Anger was a volatile emotion and it could lead people to do dramatic things. Pat hated his village being overrun with strangers, and since he lived alone, his negative emotions would have been allowed to fester in his heart. She wasn't sure why he would frame the crime to reflect something that happened to Lord Huntingdon's family, but she wasn't ready to dismiss him as a suspect either. She found his comments about Constable Dudley interesting too. Was Pat the killer and thought he was smarter than the local law, or was he right and Constable Dudley did verge on the side of incompetence. If that was the case then Lily had to work hard to ensure that she was not the one who ended up as the prime suspect.

Her next stop had to be the camp where the crew was set up.

The mood around the camp was somber. People were sitting around with long faces, sharing stories of Howard. There was a lot of uncertainty as well. The equipment stood unused, the cameras were pointed to the ground and covered with tarpaulin. The director was the lynchpin of the production, especially out here away from the studio. He had the vision and the command, and now everyone was going to be aimless. Lily smiled awkwardly at her old colleagues and friends, but made a beeline for Rick's trailer. He was the one who would know what was going on, and he was also a suspect himself. In fact most people in the camp were suspects considering what Howard had put them through.

She reached his trailer and knocked on the door, although there was no answer.

"He's on a call to the producers, trying to find out what the heck is going to happen now," Doug said. The camera man was standing by a chest filled with equipment with wires wrapped around his hands. "I'm just trying to keep busy."

Lily nodded. "How is everyone?"

"Pretty shaken up, as you can imagine. It's pretty crazy what's going on. I'm not sure any of us can actually believe it."

"I know how you feel. What actually happened? What was he doing up there?"

Doug shrugged. "I don't know. We went up to the house to scout it out yesterday afternoon. I guess he wanted to have another look at it at night. You know what he's like. Sometimes he gets an idea in his head and he just goes and follows it. It's not like anyone can tell him no."

"Yeah, I remember," Lily agreed. "Did you go with him the second time?"

Doug shook his head. "Just the first. Last night I was asleep. I don't know what happened around here. If anyone did go with him they're not talking. People were pretty tired due to the jet lag and setting up camp though.

I don't know if anyone would have been aware of anything happening. People are pretty freaked out though, you know, at the thought that one of us is a murderer."

"You seem pretty calm."

"I'm just trying to keep busy. I don't really think it's anyone here. I think it's someone local. You saw the way that guy reacted yesterday. I wouldn't be surprised if Howard encountered someone else who was out late at night and got into an argument with them. He was lucky yesterday that he had Rick and me to pull him away. It's always the way with these things, isn't it? He was in the wrong place at the wrong time."

Lily nodded. Perhaps it was just that simple, although the cogs in her mind were turning. Was it possible that Howard had gone off on his own in a strange town to scout a location and ran into someone who had killed him? He was often the type of person to go off on a whim, but he was also a professional. She wasn't sure what he would have achieved by going to see a location in the dead of night. Doug walked away, carrying the bundle of wires with him, and she turned back to the trailer to knock on it again. This time the door was flung open and Rick was standing there with a look of thunder on his face.

"What do you want?" he asked tersely. There were shadows under his eyes and he radiated fury.

"I just… I want to talk about what happened. I want to try and figure this out," Lily said.

Rick rolled his eyes and let her into the trailer. He turned around and poured himself a glass of whiskey, offering her one, but she declined.

"I don't mean to shout at you," he said. "I've just been on the phone with the producers trying to figure out what the heck we're going to do about this film. They've sunk so much money in already they don't want to just write it off, but we just lost the director." He slammed the drink back and wiped his lips. "I always wondered why Howard was in such a bad mood, now I'm starting to realize why. So what are you doing here?"

"I'm trying to find out what happened. I'm writing a murder mystery and I thought I could lend my expertise. Plus I knew him… I feel like I should do *something*."

"Well I'm not sure there's much you can do," Rick said.

"What is going to happen with the film?" Lily asked.

"They said they're going to try and salvage it when we get back to America, but they want us to continue here. I think they're going to get me to take over from where Howard left off. No doubt he'll be rolling in his grave at the thought that I'm going to direct his picture. He never thought actors were good for anything other than standing there and looking pretty."

"You did have your fair share of arguments," Lily said. Rick's demeanor changed immediately. He glared at her and his tone turned icy.

"Yeah, we did, but it always led to great art, and that's what mattered in the end. Things aren't going to be the same without him. There were times when I hated him, but I never stopped respecting him. Now I have to figure out how to deal with this," he closed his eyes and pressed his hand against his forehead. There was a moment where Lily pitied him, but then she remembered that he was an actor and displaying false emotions was his trade. Looking at things objectively, Rick was one of the people who benefitted from Howard's death. Now he was given a promotion to direct the film, an opportunity that Howard would never have given him. Was there some motivation there? Had Rick gone to Howard and asked him for a chance to direct, and upon Howard's refusal had Rick's anger gotten the better of him?

She had already seen him feign emotion with Pat, and he certainly looked as though he hadn't gotten much sleep. Was this from a guilty conscience? After all, Doug had already told her that most people in the camp had slept soundly. It struck her as odd that Rick was sleep deprived.

She sidled closer to the door, ready for a quick escape just in case Rick was the murderer. Icy fear ran down her spine and her skin tingled. Her throat tightened and went dry as she realized she might be in close proximity with a killer. She was supposed to be a writer. These situations were supposed to be abstract concepts, but here she was, right in the thick of it.

"I don't suppose you noticed anyone going off with Howard last night, did you?" as she asked this she had to use all her willpower to keep her voice from trembling.

"No, I didn't. I couldn't focus on anything apart from that rooster going off all night. I thought they were supposed to cry at the crack of dawn. This one must have been blind because we couldn't sleep at all. It's the last thing we needed after the long flight."

"*Nobody* could sleep?" Lily asked, surprised because it went against what Doug had said.

"Not for a good while. I guess Howard had trouble sleeping as well and that's why he went off by himself. I didn't pay much attention to who was moving about the camp though. There were a few people who got up during the night, but I think most of us stayed in our trailers and tried to bury our heads in the pillow to drown out the rooster. Thankfully it eventually stopped so I managed to get a few hours' sleep, although I don't know how I'm going to sleep tonight." He ran his hand through his hair and looked aggrieved, but Lily's mind was already elsewhere.

"I have to go," she said, suddenly feeling a spark of inspiration, mixed with fear. Her heart thrummed for she felt as though she knew who had committed the murder, but there was still the matter of catching him.

CHAPTER FIVE

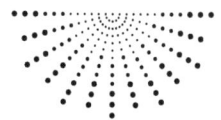

There were many people who could have committed the murder, including Lily herself, but she thought she had narrowed it down. She just needed proof now. She walked around camp, searching for Doug because what he told her made no sense. Why would he think that everyone was sleeping soundly if he had been in the camp, unless he wasn't in the camp at all during the time the rooster was squawking? Her footsteps were quick as she rushed through the camp, making her way to one of the large tents that had been erected to house the equipment. She found Doug there, standing in front of a camera, scrubbing it vigorously.

There were various types of cameras used on a film set. There were the huge standing ones that took in most of the action, but there were also smaller ones that camera men carried on their shoulders, and this was the type that Doug was cleaning.

"Doug, what are you doing?" she asked warily.

Doug paused for a moment before he turned around. His lips were thin and even, while his eyes were dark and brooding. There was something chilling about his expression, and Lily's mouth ran dry.

"I'm just keeping busy, you know, to take my mind off things," he said. Lily angled her head to try and get a better look at the camera, but as she did so Doug turned his body to prevent her from seeing it properly. "What are you still doing here? I would have thought it would be too depressing to be around a place like this.

You should head back to your cottage, get some rest."

"I think I'd rather be here," Lily said. "There's something that I've been wondering about Doug... you told me that everyone was asleep. Wasn't there anything that disturbed people during the night?"

"Not that I know of."

"That's funny Doug, because I was just talking to Rick and he said that there was a rooster crying out for a while that woke everyone up. But if you didn't hear it then..."

"I guess I'm a heavy sleeper."

"Or you weren't here at all," she said. As soon as the words slipped out of her mouth she knew that something was wrong with Doug. The bland expression changed on his face and he suddenly looked like a monster. Before she could move he had burst across the tent toward her and grabbed the bundle of wires he had carried with him earlier. She twisted away, trying to run, but his arms were already around her. The wires dragged around her throat and he started pulling tighter and tighter, and the world was growing darker and darker…

"You shouldn't have poked your nose in here. You should have left and kept your distance. This isn't your world anymore. It's not your problem." Doug spoke through gritted teeth as he tried to choke the life out of her. Lily gasped and gagged and flailed everything she had to try and escape. In one brusque movement she managed to stomp on his foot and for a moment his grip was released. It was only one brief moment, but she made it count. She screamed at the top of her lungs for help. Doug's hand came over her mouth almost immediately, suffocating her, and he pulled the wires even tauter.

She always feared that Hollywood would be the death of her, and she hated to be proven right. The strength slipped from her body and she began to lose the will to resist.

Then, just as he had done in so many movies, Rick Chambers came charging in, along with others from the crew who had heard the scream. They wrestled Doug off her and she fell to the ground, gasping for air and clutching her throat.

"What the heck is going on here?" Rick asked.

"I don't know! She went crazy! I think she was the one who did it. I think she killed Howard!" Doug exclaimed. Lily's eyes went wide with panic. She coughed and spluttered, trying to protest her innocence, but it was so hard to speak. Her neck blazed with pain, but she pointed to the camera and managed to utter a single word, directing Rick's eyes to the device.

He frowned for a moment as he tried to understand her, and then he followed her guidance to look at the camera. The moment he did so, he recoiled in shock.

"There's blood on here! There's blood!" he cried, and Doug roared in anguish.

EPILOGUE

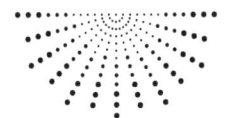

"It's all been rather exciting here, hasn't it?" Marjorie said, placing a few sweet treats in a bag. Lily went to pay, but Marjorie shook her head and insisted she do no such thing. "I couldn't ask you to pay, not after what you did."

"I didn't really do all that much. I only asked a few questions," Lily said.

"Nonsense! You put yourself in harm's way. You're very brave Lily. I daresay I couldn't have done what you did. And you solved the crime before Constable Dudley managed to.

What was it like? Did you find out why he killed the director?"

Lily nodded. The moments after Rick had seen the blood on the camera had been fraught with tension. Doug knew the game was up and he had confessed to everything. "Doug has been working with Howard for a long time, and because he's a cameraman he's seen everything. I think he just had had enough. He said that Howard dragged him out of bed last night to go and scout the location under the moonlight, which Doug didn't like because he was trying to sleep. Apparently Howard was running his mouth and insulted Doug, and Doug let his anger get the better of him. He hit Doug with the camera, and the impact was hard enough to kill him. Doug was trying to clean the evidence off the camera before anyone could find out what had happened, but he was too late."

"So there was nothing to the fact that it happened in the same manner as the old story?" Marjorie asked.

"Just coincidence I think, although I'm going to want to hear more about that story next time I come in here. I've only heard the basics."

"You're welcome any time Lily, any time at all," Marjorie said.

Lily thanked her for the sweet treats and returned to Starling Cottage, where Joanie was waiting for her. Lily handed her the bag and Joanie smiled with glee as she smelled the delicious treats.

"Are you sure you don't mind me staying for a while? I think this is a sign that I should take a break from Hollywood too," Joanie said.

Lily was slightly annoyed at having her peaceful idyll broken, but she couldn't be too despondent about her friend asking to stay. She would be glad for the company. The film crew was packing up already, eager to leave the sorry business behind them. Once it was revealed that a member of the crew was responsible for Howard's death there was no way the film could continue, so the peaceful town of Didlington St. Wilfried was left alone again. The flash of excitement was over.

"I promise you that it's not like this all the time," Lily said. "Most of the time it's perfectly relaxing. I think it's time I get back to writing my book," she said, and bid Joanie farewell. Lily retired to her study where she sat down in front of her computer and reviewed what she had written so far. She ended up changing much of the story out of respect for Howard. For all the hostility that had existed between them she hadn't thought he deserved to die, and she didn't want to appear as though she was taking advantage of his tragic death. But she was sure that in her book as in real life justice would be done, and she felt a sense of pride in the role she had played.

She was also glad that she had managed to solve the crime quickly, as Constable Dudley had revealed to her in a joking manner that she had been his prime suspect. It was a chilling thought to know how close she had come to being arrested, and she vowed to never take inspiration from real life again, or at least to have an iron clad alibi if she did.

A little while later she was disturbed by Joanie shouting from the lounge, telling her that someone was at the door. Lily rolled her eyes and wondered what this was about. Surely there couldn't have been another murder!

But as she emerged from her study she saw a strapping man standing in the doorway. It was as though he had been plucked from one of her dreams.

"I'm Blake Huntingdon," he said, "after the recent events I thought it best to check on my father's property." His voice was a low, rumbling baritone. Lily and Joanie were both swooning. Life in Didlington St. Wilfried was surprising indeed. She never knew what was going to turn up on her doorstep.

THANK YOU FOR CHOOSING A PUREREAD BOOK!

We hope you enjoyed the story, and as a way to thank you for choosing PureRead we'd like to send you this free Special Edition Cozy, and other fun reader rewards...

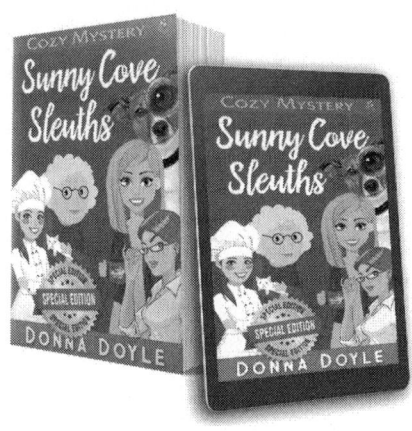

Click Here to download your free Cozy Mystery PureRead.com/cozy

Thanks again for reading.
See you soon!

WHAT'S NEXT FOR LILY?

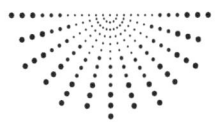

Hot on the heels of this hot Hollywood mystery Lily's adventures in Didlington do not stop. This time she must defend one of her new friends from horrible accusations of poisoning a parishioner…

Here's the first chapter of A Perfect Poisoned Pastry In A Quiet English Village for your enjoyment.

DEADLY DELICIOUS

"I'm glad that excitement is all over with," Frank Roberts said as Marjorie deposited some of her sweet treats into a bag and handed them to him. Frank was a man of average height with a face as round as the moon, and a smile as wide as the heavens above.

"I don't know about that; it was nice to have a change of pace around here," Marjorie replied.

"I moved here for a change of pace! The best thing about Didlington St. Wilfrid is that nothing happens. The beauty lies in the peace."

"It seems a lot of people are coming here for a change of pace," Marjorie said.

Frank arched an eyebrow. He knew who she was talking about. "How is our newest star in the making? I have to admit I'm not entirely convinced that an American fits in well here."

Marjorie gave him an admonishing look. "Lily McGee is one of the sweetest women I've ever met and if it wasn't for her all that terrible business with the murder would never have been solved. She's a wonderful woman and you would be blessed to know her."

Frank raised his hands, surprised at the force of the words. But Marjorie was the kind of woman who defended her friends with all the strength she could muster.

"I stand corrected," Frank said with a wry smile. "I would be a fool to ignore your judgment. Perhaps our paths will cross. After all, it's a small village."

"And if she takes a liking to you perhaps she'll put you in one of her books," Marjorie wore a teasing smile.

Frank shuddered and grimaced. "I don't know about that. I'm not sure how I'd feel about someone putting words into my mouth or making me do things that I have no control over, even if it's not really me they're controlling."

"I think you're thinking too much into it. Lily has already said she's going to base a character on me in her next book," Marjorie let out a little squeal of excitement.

"Well I'm sure that the character will be charming and beautiful," Frank said warmly.

Marjorie's cheeks glowed. "Get on with you," she said, waving a playful hand toward him. "Charlotte will be wondering where you are."

Frank sighed and arched his eyebrows. "Yes, that she will," he said with a sense of burden weighing upon him, the burden that came with marriage. He stood there for a moment and his gaze drifted to the pictures hanging on the wall, depicting her late husband. "Can I ask you something Marjorie? Did you and Henry ever have times when… well… when you wondered if you should have gotten married in the first place?"

The smile fell from Marjorie's face, replaced by a gleaming sorrow in her eyes as they turned liquid. Frank immediately felt ashamed for causing such a reaction in her.

"I think marriage is a journey, and on that journey there are always moments of doubt, but it's important to remember that those moments do not define the journey. Are you and Charlotte…?" she trailed off at the end, unable to bring herself to ask the question directly, but Frank knew what was implied.

He nodded and ran his hand along his bare chin, suddenly looking as though he had aged a decade in a matter of moments. "There are times when I look at her and I just think that she's not the woman I married," he said.

"I'm sure things will get better," Marjorie said. "And while you're having these problems you know that I'm always here for a chat, but you should probably get back to her. The only way you're going to get close to her is to be with her."

"Yes, you're probably right," Frank said. He thanked Marjorie and left the warm, cloying heat of the bakery. The door closed behind him, and he left Marjorie gazing at the picture of her husband. Frank thought it was a tragedy that a marriage should have ended so swiftly, but he wished his own wasn't plagued by trouble. Recently Charlotte had been… difficult. It was hard to describe to be honest, and he wasn't even sure how long it had been going on. The years had a way of blurring into each other. One blink and suddenly a boy was a man, with fewer years ahead than he had behind him, leaving ragged hopes and dreams for someone else to pick up.

He heard the bark of a dog as Zeus approached him. Frank crossed the road, never having been the kind of man who appreciated the company of canines. The appearance of Zeus also meant that Pat wouldn't be too far behind, and the less Frank had to do with Pat the better. In the dim light of the evening he looked across the road. Pat glared at him as he glared at everyone, for no apparent reason. Frank's skin crawled. Pat was the kind of man who carried threat with him, and Frank was glad when Pat continued on his way. Frank found himself walking more rapidly to his house, which happened to neighbor Pat's farm.

His small cottage was a cozy place, like something out of a fairytale. He paused for a moment before he entered, taking a deep breath and promising himself that tonight would be a special night for himself and Charlotte. Something caught his eye on the doorstep, a smooth envelope that looked as though it should have been pushed through the letterbox. He bent down to pick it up and was surprised to find that there was no address written on the envelope and no stamp. He unsealed the envelope and pulled out a single sheet of plain paper. The letters were large, and it appeared as though the ink had been slashed across the page.

"Your sins will find you out. Do you really have a death wish?"

Frank stared at the words, unsure of their meaning, but fear curdled in the pit of his stomach. He scrunched up the letter and shoved it in his pocket, ignoring the crawling sensation that ran up and down the back of his neck.

The smell of roasted meat and thick gravy greeted him as he entered. Charlotte was standing in the kitchen with her arms folded across her chest and her eyes as cold as ice. Her features were sharp, and her black hair formed a midnight veil across her face.

"You're late," she said, the words cutting through the air. Frank's heart sank. So it was going to be one of *those* nights.

"Yes, I just stopped off at the bakery to pick us up some dessert," Frank said, lifting the bag he had brought back from Marjorie's. At the mention of it Charlotte rolled her eyes.

"Of course you did. Any excuse to go and spend time with *her*," Charlotte spat.

Frank sighed and pinched the bridge of his nose. "Let's not do this again Charlotte, please."

"We wouldn't have to do it again if you didn't keep making a point of going to see her."

"She owns the bakery Charlotte, besides, this place is so small it's not like I can actually avoid anyone," his voice was strained, but he managed to keep himself from shouting.

"You could if you tried. I've seen the way she looks at you. You're this handsome stranger who came from the glamorous city. She's lonely, and lonely women do desperate things. You don't think I see what she's doing? She's plying you with all these sweet treats, fattening you up like a turkey for Christmas."

"Charlotte, you're really overreacting. We're just friends. We have a little chat when I buy something from her bakery. There's nothing going on, believe me. I'm married to you. I brought this treat back so that we could share it."

"I don't want to eat anything that's been touched by her hands," Charlotte said bitterly. Frank's head dropped, for he didn't know what to do. His stomach growled so he went to the table and began eating. Charlotte dropped down to the table as well, joining him in the meal. It was a strange meal though, silent and tense and Charlotte never took her gaze off him. There were so many things he wanted to say, yet he wasn't sure how to begin. It seemed as though anything he said was going to turn into an argument anyway, so perhaps it was better not to say anything at all.

But then, Frank had never been the kind of man to avoid a problem until it was too late.

"I think we need to talk Charlotte, about us."

"I knew it," she said. "I knew there was something going on with you and that baker."

"There's not Charlotte, and I don't like how you can even believe that there is."

"You can't blame me," Charlotte said, and the look that flashed in her eyes made Frank swallow a lump in his throat. For a moment he was filled with shame.

Frank chose his next words carefully, keeping his voice measured, speaking in between chewing the tender meat and the delicious vegetables. "We came here to move on Charlotte. We were supposed to find our happy ending here, away from the distractions of the city, but we're not going to be able to do that if we keep living in the past. We have to look to the future and to the life that we could have together."

Charlotte's voice was rasping when she replied. Her hands trembled and glistening lines trickled down her cheeks. "You're acting as though this is my fault Frank. I've given you everything. I've tried *everything*. I came out here for you. I left my friends and my family for you and this place, but nothing has changed really, has it? We can change all the things that are around us, but we can't change ourselves."

Frank was about to say something else, but she left her meal half eaten and left the room, choking on her sobs. Frank thought about going after her, but he wasn't sure anything he said would actually do any good. It might be better for Charlotte to have some time alone.

Frank finished the food on his plate and then decided to leave the washing up until a little later. He took his sweet treat into the lounge and settled into a plush leather chair, telling himself that he shouldn't let this argument ruin his enjoyment of the night. He still had to get his happiness after all, although in a way that had been the problem that had brought their lives to this quaint village. But Frank wanted to be a better man. He wanted to be a good husband, it was just that sometimes it was *so* hard.

As he opened the bag and pulled out the éclair he thought about Marjorie, how sweet and friendly she was. She had a kind of homespun beauty that would not have been remarkable at all in the city, but it was a beauty that was imbued with a kind of strength, a strength that Charlotte could never possess. The sugary, creamy treat bathed his tongue in a wild storm of sweetness and delight, and it was almost enough to soothe his aching heart. He wondered how his life would be different if he had chosen another woman to be his wife, and he hated himself for it.

The sweetness lingered on his tongue as he sat there in the shadows of the evening, reflecting on Marjorie's words. He wondered how much truth there was to them, and how he would know when the difficult moments actually became the journey. But for now he still had the wherewithal to try and fix his marriage. They had uprooted their lives to come here so that they could be together and find their happy ever after, but Frank wasn't naïve enough to believe it would be so easy. He prepared to pull himself up and go and see his wife, but then a strange sensation overwhelmed him. His chest tightened and the world grew hazy, as though it was spinning around him. Then there was a sharp pain in his torso, which made him clutch his stomach. He leaned forward and coughed, looking with concern at the dark blood and black bile that stained his hand. It felt as though he was on fire and when he tried to call out for help, nothing but a rasping whisper escaped his lips. He lunged forward and tried to crawl toward the staircase, to get to his wife, but all his strength left him. A hacking cough brought up yet more bile, and he felt the kind of dread that came with any man's final moments.

His hand reached toward the door, toward his wife, but he knew that nobody could save him now. Tears flowed from his eyes, mixing with the blood and the bile that lingered on his lips, and then the darkness closed in. Then, there was nothing…

Continue reading A Perfect Poisoned Pastry In A Quiet English Village to find out whose behind this poisoned pastry puzzle...

Click here to read on Kindle

OTHER BOOKS IN THIS SERIES

If you loved this story why not continue straight away with other books in the series?

A Huge Hollywood Mystery In A Quiet English Village

A Perfect Poisoned Pastry In A Quiet English Village

A Freaky Family Murder In A Quiet English Village

A Sinister Stormy Crime in a Quiet English Village

A Bony Buried Secret In A Quiet English Village

A Child Goes Missing in a Quiet English Village

Corpse in a Crypt in a Quiet English Village

A Frightfully Foggy Mystery in a Quiet English Village

A Sneaky Sibling Mystery in a Quiet English Village

A Cooked Up Crime in a Quiet English Village

Who Killed the Colonel in a Quiet English Village

OUR GIFT TO YOU

AS A WAY TO SAY THANK YOU WE WOULD LOVE TO SEND YOU THIS SPECIAL EDITION COZY MYSTERY FREE OF CHARGE.

Our Reader List is 100% FREE

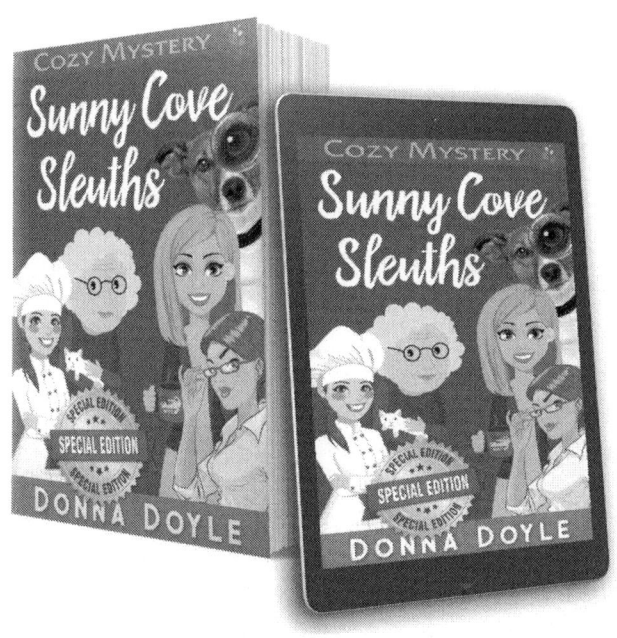

Click Here to download your free Cozy Mystery **PureRead.com/cozy**

At PureRead we publish books you can trust. Great tales without smut or swearing, but with all of the mystery and romance you expect from a great story.

Be the first to know when we release new books, take part in our fun competitions, and get surprise free books in your inbox by signing up to our Reader list.

As a thank you you'll receive this exclusive Special Edition Cozy available only to our subscribers...

Click Here to download your free Cozy Mystery **PureRead.com/cozy**

Thanks again for reading.
See you soon!

Made in the USA
Columbia, SC
21 January 2024